MONSTER MASH

DAVID CATROW

ORCHARD BOOKS

AN IMPRINT OF SCHOLASTIC INC.
NEW YORK

I was working in the lab late one night,
when my eyes beheld an eerie sight.

WHIP BLEND MUTE ON
PUREE

For my monster from his slab began to rise,
and suddenly, to my surprise . . .

He did the mash.
He did the monster mash!
The monster mash.
It was a graveyard smash.

He did the **mash.**
It caught on in a flash.

He did the **mash.**
He did the **monster mash!**

From my laboratory in the castle east
to the master bedroom where the vampires feast,
the ghouls all came from their humble abodes
to get a jolt from my electrodes.

They did the mash.
They did the monster mash!
The monster mash.
It was a graveyard smash.
They did the mash.
It caught on in a flash.
They did the mash.
They did the monster mash!

The zombies were having fun.
The party had just begun.
The guests included Wolf Man,
Dracula, and his son.

The scene was rocking.
All were digging the sounds:
Igor on chains,
backed by his baying hounds.

The coffin-bangers
were about to arrive
with their vocal group,
The Crypt-Kicker Five.

They played the **mash**.
They played the **monster mash**.
The **monster mash**.
It was a graveyard smash.
They played the **mash**.
It caught on in a flash.
They played the **mash**.
They played the **monster mash**!

Out from his coffin,
Drac's voice did ring.
Seems he was troubled
by just one thing.

He opened the lid and shook his fist and said,
"Whatever happened to my Transylvania twist?"

It's now the **mash.**
It's now the **monster mash!**
The **monster mash.**
And it's a graveyard smash.

It's now the **mash**.
It's caught on in a flash.
It's now the **mash**.
It's now the **monster** mash!

Now everything's cool—
Drac's a part of the band.
And my monster mash
is the hit of the land.

For you, the living,
this **mash** was meant, too.
When you get to my door,
tell them Boris sent you!

Then you can mash.
Then you can monster mash!
The monster mash.
And do my graveyard smash.

Then you can mash.
You'll catch on in a flash.
Then you can mash.
Then you can monster mash!

For all the little monsters — D.C.

Words and Music by Bobby Pickett and Leonard Capizzi
© 1962 (renewed) FSMGI (IMRO), Gary S. Paxton Publications (BMI), and Capizzi Music Co. (BMI) (c/o Serling, Rooks & Ferrara, LLP)
All rights for FSMGI (IMRO) and Gary S. Paxton Publications (BMI) administered by State One Music America (BMI)
Used by permission of Alfred Music Publishing Co., Inc.

Illustrations copyright © 2012 by David Catrow

Library of Congress Cataloging-in-Publication Data
Catrow, David.
Monster mash / David Catrow.—1st ed. p. cm.
Summary: In this illustrated version of the classic novelty song, a mad scientist's monster performs a new dance which becomes "the hit of the land" when the scientist throws a party for other monsters.
ISBN 978-0-545-21479-7
1. Children's songs, English—United States—Texts. [1. Monsters—Songs and music. 2. Dance—Songs and music. 3. Songs.] I. Title. PZ8.3.C29Mo 2012 782.42—dc23 [E] 2011034406

10 9 8 7 6 5 4 3 2 1   12 13 14 15 16
Printed in Singapore 46
First edition, July 2012

The display type was set in P22 Kane Regular.
The text was set in 16 pt. Senza Black TDI.
The art was created using pencil, watercolor, gouache, and ink.
Book design by Marijka Kostiw

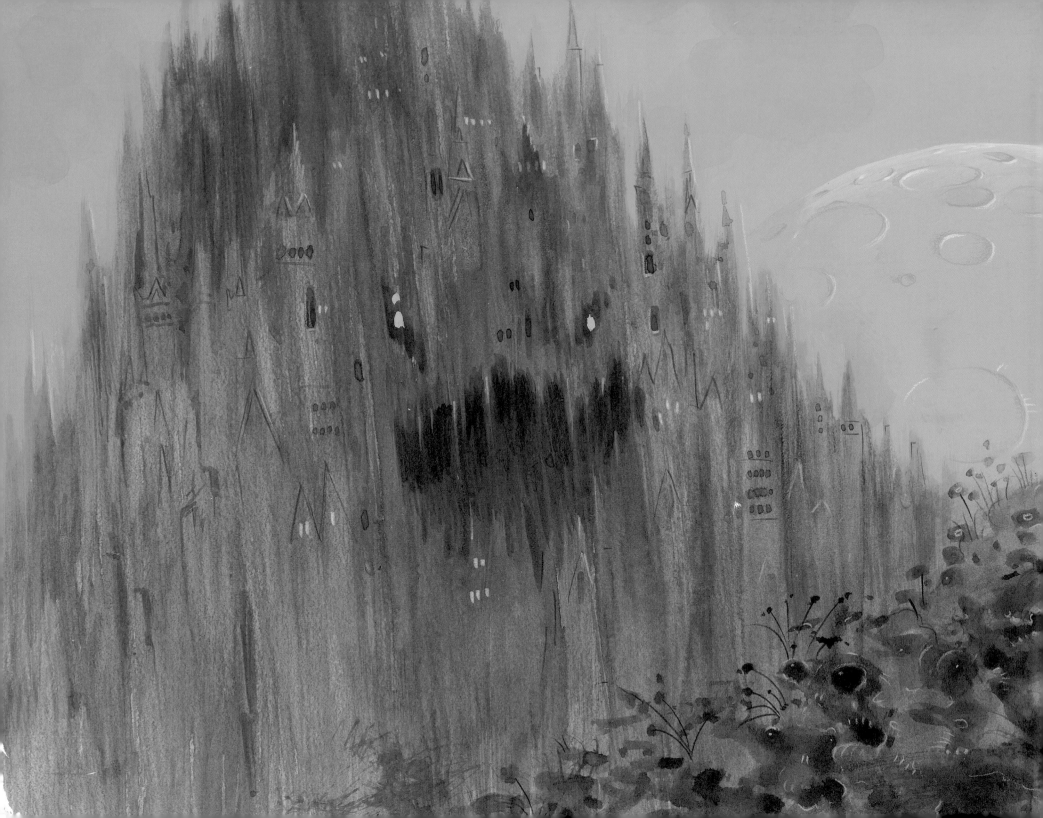